MAR 2017

PERCY
DOG OF DESTINY

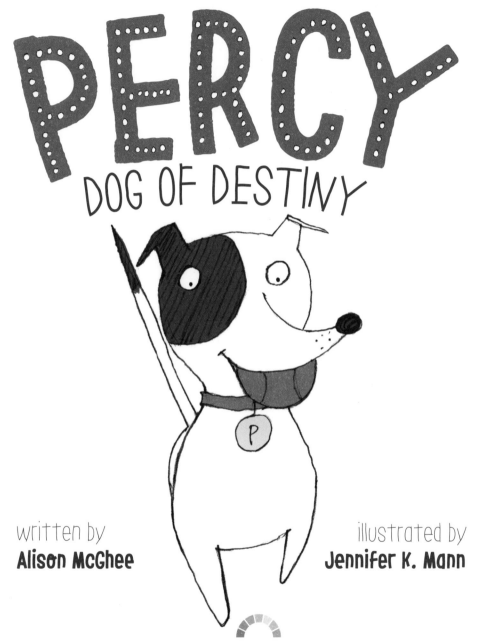

written by
Alison McGhee

illustrated by
Jennifer K. Mann

BOYDS MILLS PRESS
AN IMPRINT OF HIGHLIGHTS
Honesdale, Pennsylvania

For my lovely, dog-loving friend Judy Osborn,
whose work with the VetDog program is inspirational. —*AM*

This is dedicated to the memory of our dog-boy Dayo,
and his cheerful determination to have a ball in action
for as many minutes of the day as possible. —*JKM*

Boyds Mills Press
An Imprint of Highlights
815 Church Street
Honesdale, Pennsylvania 18431

Printed in China
ISBN: 978-1-59078-984-1
Library of Congress Control Number: 2016942356

First edition
Jacket design by Marie O'Neill
Book design by Sara Gillingham Studio
Production by Sue Cole
The text of this book is set in Bodoni Egyptian Pro®.
The illustrations are done in pencil and digital paint.

10 9 8 7 6 5 4 3 2 1

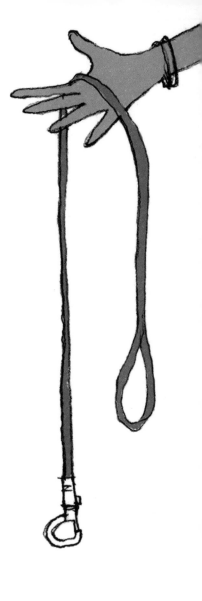

Dog park?
What ho!

Where's my special ball?

There you are,
my little porkie pie.

Make way, world.

The Dog of Destiny and his ball
are heading to the dog park!

Here's Molly and her kerchief.

Oatmeal Raisin Cookie and her Frisbee.

And Fluffy and his bone.

What ho!

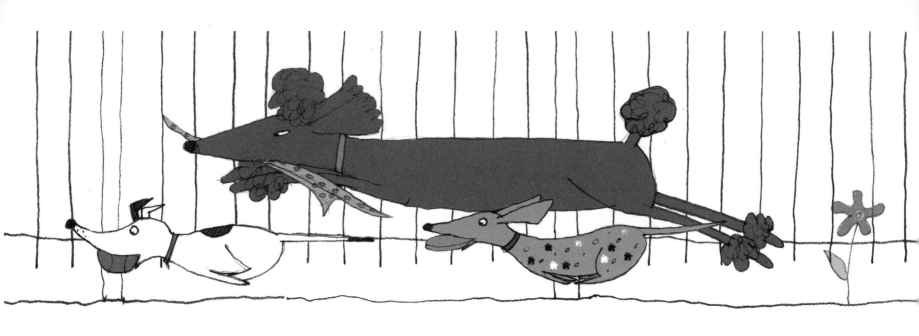

Time to streak along the fence.

Oh, Fluffy.

Time to do some sniffing.

Oh, Fluffy.

Time to dig some holes.

Oh, Fluffy.

Time to pee on the tree.

Oh, Fluffy.

What have we here?

If it isn't a squirrel.

You call that a ball,
squirrel?

This is a ball!

The squirrel wants my ball.
I can tell.

No one can have my ball.
It's mine, mine, mine!

Time to teach this squirrel a lesson.
Are we dogs, or are we doughnuts?

Come, Molly.

Now, Cookie.

Fluffy, where are you?

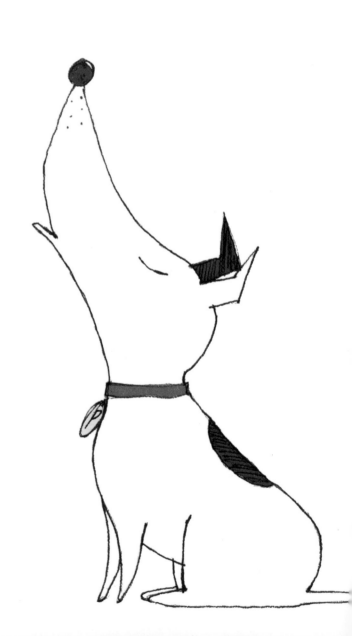

Oh, Fluffy.

MY

BALL!

Precious!

Cupcake!

Little porkie pie!
Sweet poopsie muffin,
come to papa!

Oh, Fluffy!

FLUFFY!

What ho!